# WILLIE WISH GRANTER

## Wilma's Wish

Wished & Written
by
Wayne E. Hoffman

Illustrated by Kalpart

williewishgranter.com

There is no limitations on wishes, and no wrong way to wish...

The outcome of wishes made rests in the heart and eyes of the Wish maker.

~ Willie Wish Granter

# Introduction

Have you ever made a wish?

I have too.

What did you wish for?

WAIT! Don't tell me,

It may not come true.

# How did you wish?

-    A four-leaf clover

-    A Thanksgiving Wishbone

-    Flipping a coin into a well

-    A star in the nights sky

-    Or simply saying...

# I WISH?

# But, WHO did you wish to?

Now, most people if asked, would say that they wish to GOD.

Others may say that GOD hears our prayers, not our wishes.

And then others will just say "I don't know".

What if I told you that GOD has helpers for all aspects of life

Such as:

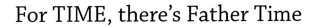

For TIME, there's Father Time

For WEATHER, there's Mother Nature

SLEEP... The Sand Man

LOVE... Cupid

The Tooth Fairy

The EASTER BUNNY

SANTA...

# Well, what about WISHING?

I wish for a puppy,
I wish for a pony,
I wish I had some cheese macaroni.

8

I wish all day,

I wish all night,

I wish, I wish, with all of my might.

9

I wish for a monkey,

I wish for a fish,

Oh me, Oh my... I wish, I wish, I wish.

I wish on a birthday cake,

I wish on a four-leaf clover,

I wish, I wish...

over and over.

I wish silently in my head,

Or I whisper into the air,

Anyway, anyhow...

Someone special will overhear.

Wishes can be fun,

Wishes can be silly,

Wishes can be heard,

IF YOU WISH TO WILLIE.

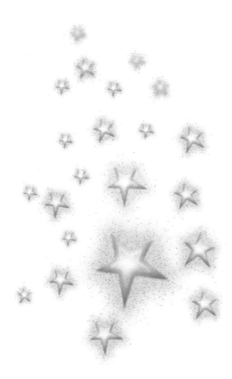

# Once upon a time

## Not so long ago,

People would make wishes,

And not know where those wishes would go.

And then one day,

Someone decided to ask,

Willie wished up to the stars,

And he took on that task.

16

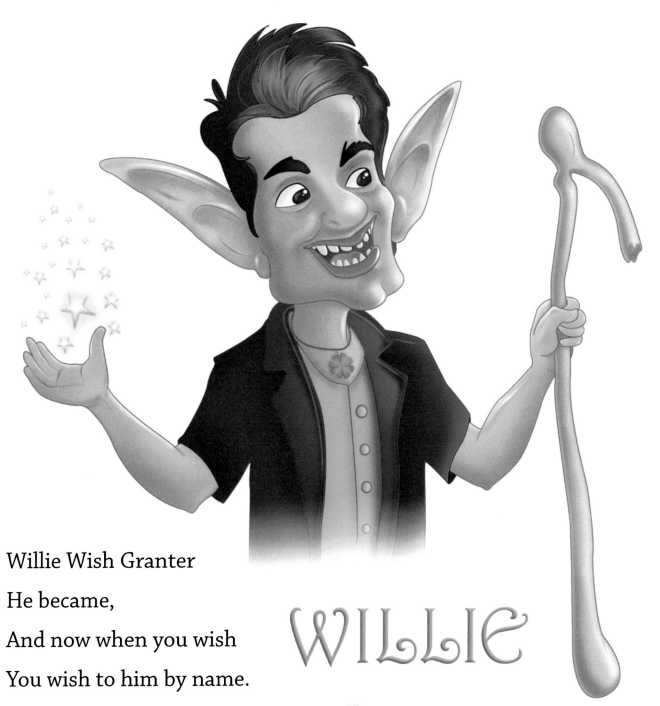

Willie Wish Granter
He became,
And now when you wish
You wish to him by name.

WILLIE

Willies ears sprouted,
Willies toes tingle,
Every time someone wishes,
Willie hears a jingle.

18

Willie Listens,

Willie hears,

Willie grants wishes,

Because Willie cares.

19

Willie hears wishes every day,
Willie knows people wish in every way.

People wish to a star in the night,
They wish on a four-leaf clover with all of their might,
We blow out birthday candles with all of our gust,
While wishing on 11:11 is an absolute must,
Some flip a penny into a well,
For others a Thanksgiving wishbone may ring a bell,
We blow on a dandelion until the seeds run dry,
Or when a single feather falls from the sky.

Our wishes to be granted,

Is what we wish to achieve,

We wish over and over...

Because in Willie

We believe.

One day Willie heard a jingle,

And he listened with glee,

And that was when Wilma's wish,

Came to be.

Now this has never
happened before,

And caught Willie by
surprise,

But this wish,
Wilma's wish...

Willie heard with his
eyes.

23

Wilma was upbeat and positive,

Wilma was playful and fun,

When Willie heard her jingle,

Willie knew she was the one.

Wilma's wish was simple,

Wilma's wish was small,

Wilma wished that someone could hear her...

Anyone at all.

Willie wanted so badly,

To make Wilma's wish come true,

So, Willie Yelled and He screamed...

I'm listening to you.

26

Willie wanted to grant Wilma's wish,

He wanted to answer Wilma's call,

But Willie realized he was already listening,

So, it wasn't a wish at all.

Wilma felt different,
Wilma felt heard,
Wilma felt comfort,
In the unspoken word.

28

Wilma felt Willies presence,

Which gave a feeling she would keep,

She thanked Willie Wish Granter,

And then she went to sleep.

# The End

Made in the USA
Monee, IL
26 October 2020